MOONBEAR'S SKYFIRE

A MOONBEAR Book

· FRANK ASCH ·

ALADDIN

NEW YORK   LONDON   TORONTO   SYDNEY   NEW DELHI

ALADDIN

An imprint of Simon & Schuster Children's Publishing Division
1230 Avenue of the Americas, New York, NY 10020
This Aladdin edition March 2014
Copyright © 1984 by Frank Asch

ALADDIN is a trademark of Simon & Schuster, Inc., and related logo is
a registered trademark of Simon & Schuster, Inc.
For information about special discounts for bulk purchases, please contact
Simon & Schuster Special Sales at 1-866-506-1949 or business@simonandschuster.com.
The Simon & Schuster Speakers Bureau can bring authors to your live event.
For more information or to book an event contact the Simon & Schuster Speakers Bureau
at 1-866-248-3049 or visit our website at www.simonspeakers.com.
Designed by Karina Granda and Karin Paprocki
The text of this book was set in Olympian LT Std.
Manufactured in China 1213 SCP
10 9 8 7 6 5 4 3 2 1
The Library of Congress has cataloged a previous edition as follows:
Asch, Frank. Skyfire / by Frank Asch
cm.
Summary: When he sees a rainbow for the first time, Bear thinks that
the sky is on fire and he is determined to put out the skyfire.
[1. Rainbow—Fiction. 2. Bears—Fiction.] I. Title
PZ7.A7782Sk 1998
[E]'dc19 88-3139 CIP AC
ISBN 978-1-4424-9410-7 (hc)
ISBN 978-1-4424-9409-1 (pbk)
ISBN 978-1-4424-9411-4 (eBook)

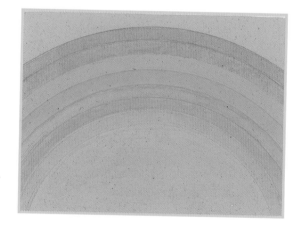

To Fred Levy

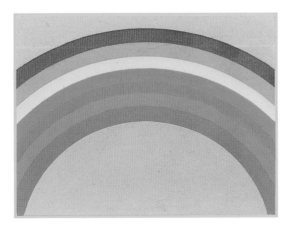

One day Bear looked out his window and saw a rainbow.

He had never seen a rainbow before.

To Bear it looked like the sky was on fire.

"Oh my goodness!" called Bear to his friend Little Bird. "Just look at the sky!"

Little Bird flew over to Bear's window.

"Why, it's a rainbow!" said Little Bird. "Come on! Let's go find the pot of gold."

"Pot of gold?" said Bear. "What are you talking about?"

"Don't you know?" replied Little Bird. "They say there's a pot of gold at the end of the rainbow."

"What nonsense!" said Bear. "The sky is on fire and all you can talk about is gold!"

And he picked up an empty honey pot and ran outside.

At the pond Bear filled the pot with water.

Then he ran toward the rainbow.

He ran and he ran and he ran.

"Look, Bear," said Little Bird,

"the rainbow ends right by that hollow tree."

But Bear wasn't listening. He was busy climbing a hill.
When he got to the top, he threw water at the rainbow.

Just then the rainbow faded away.

Little Bird chirped, "Look, Bear, I found the gold."

Bear went to the tree.

Inside he found lots of *golden* honey.

He filled his pot . . .

and took it home.

That night Little Bird came over.

Bear made honey cakes.

After dinner they went for a boat ride.

For a long while they were very quiet.

Then Little Bird said, "So it *was* a rainbow, and I found the pot of gold!"

"Oh, no, it wasn't," replied Bear. "It was a skyfire . . .

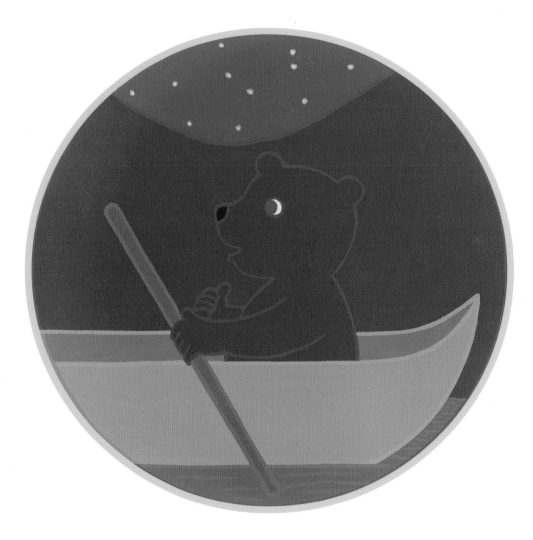

and I put it out!"